MENACE AT THE CHRISTMAS MARKET

MENACE AT THE CHRISTMAS MARKET

A NOVELLA IN THE MURDER ON LOCATION SERIES

SARA ROSETT

MENACE AT THE CHRISTMAS MARKET: A NOVELLA
Book Five in the *Murder on Location* series
An English Village Murder Mystery
Published by McGuffin Ink

First Paperback Edition: October 2016
ISBN: 978-0-9982535-4-1
Cover Design: James at GoOnWrite.com

❀ Created with Vellum

ABOUT MENACE AT THE CHRISTMAS MARKET

A NOVELLA IN THE MURDER ON LOCATION SERIES

With the Christmas holidays nearing, Kate has time off, a rare occurrence for a location scout. The Jane Austen documentary series is in a production lull, and she plans to spend her time searching for the perfect Christmas gift for Alex, which has turned out to be a task as difficult as finding an unspoiled location for a medieval-inspired fantasy series. Kate goes to the local Regency-themed Christmas Market in search of a gift, but while she's there a new acquaintance meets with foul play. Kate is drawn into the investigation and soon realizes she must discover who wants to make sure she doesn't ring in the New Year.

"I sincerely hope your Christmas in Hertfordshire may abound in the gaieties which that season generally brings..."

—Jane Austen, *Pride and Prejudice*

CHAPTER 1

NETHER WOODSMOOR

"AND HOW ARE the Canary Islands?" I asked as I looked out the kitchen window into the sodden garden behind my cottage.

"As advertised, it is a mellow sixty-seven degrees, and there isn't a cloud in the sky." Alex's voice came through the phone clearly, sounding as if he were in the next room, not off the coast of Africa. "What is it like there?"

"Rather dreary, actually."

"Raining again?"

"Yes, but I meant the lack of company."

Alex's laugh sounded in my ear, then he dropped the volume of his voice. "Believe me, I wish I was there, too. Sun or no sun."

"So it's not going…well?" Alex didn't talk about his parents much, so my knowledge about his family was sketchy, but I did know his parents were divorced and interactions with his mother were the one thing that made his easy-going nature vanish and put him on edge. As far as I could tell, his mother didn't have a fixed address. She seemed to go wherever the sun was shining. It sounded as if she was more interested in her tan than her children—thus the Christmas visit to Gran Canaria, the largest island of the chain.

Yes, I'd looked it up on Wikipedia when Alex announced he was heading there for the holiday. Had I felt a smidgen of envy, gazing at pictures of sandy beaches and palm trees? No, of course not. Alex and I had only been dating a few months, and I certainly wasn't anxious to introduce the complication of extended families into our relationship equation. No, simply finding an appropriate Christmas gift for Alex was driving me batty, so I doubted we could handle the complexities of parental expectations and demands.

Our mothers seemed to be complete opposites. His mother disappeared off the radar for months, then suddenly demanded things of Alex, like this command visit during the holiday, while my mother had only one demand of me. She wanted me married—about five years ago. According to her calendar, she should have two grandchildren at this point.

So I hadn't felt the least bit slighted when Alex announced he had to go to the Canary Islands for a family Christmas celebration and hadn't invited me. Truthfully, I was relieved. However, looking at the beautiful tropical island did stir a twinge of homesickness for Southern California, where I had lived until last spring when I took a job as a location scout for a documentary series about Jane Austen's life. The dusty, parched hills covered with scrub were such a contrast to the lush countryside of Derbyshire that it almost seemed the two places could be on different planets.

I'd wanted a change from the congested, fast-paced lifestyle of L.A. I'd certainly gotten it. There was a reason it was so green in Nether Woodsmoor. Rain was a constant. At first, the showers had been refreshing, but after several months, I caught myself complaining a few times, just like the locals, about the irritating rain that never seemed to stop. In all fairness, it had been a wet summer. My friend Louise, the owner of the local pub, told me, "Don't worry, luv. Soon it will change to snow."

Alex said, "The atmosphere is tense, conversations are constantly misinterpreted, and everyone is mentally counting the days until we can pack our bags."

"That sounds…terrible, actually."

"It's about normal for the Norcutt family. Typical Christmas holiday."

Alex's tone was breezy, but I detected some genuine strain in his voice. "So no good holiday memories, at all?" I asked.

Alex paused, then said, "Well, the time in Malta wasn't bad."

Alex's dad worked in the U.S. diplomatic core, and Alex had moved all over the world as he grew up.

He continued, "Sophia was our nanny, and she let us bake these green sugar cookies. She called them holly cookies. We put those tiny red candies on them for the berries. That was a good time. Dad was always busy, even on holidays. He always took extra work so his staff could have time off. I understand that now. At the time it made for a really long day of waiting around for him to come back. What about you?"

"I never thought my holidays were especially jolly, but compared to yours, mine are practically a Hallmark movie. After my dad left, it was just me and my mom, but she loves to cook and entertain, so she always went way overboard and cooked too much food. Every January, I vow I'm not ever eating turkey and dressing again. She always tries to get someone to come over, too, so we usually had company." I left out the fact that my mom's invitations were usually extended to friends who had eligible bachelors for sons. My mother's matchmaking never took a holiday.

I wondered who she had lined up for next week when I flew back to Southern California. Despite telling her about Alex, she refused to believe I had a real live boyfriend. If she hadn't met him, he didn't exist. I knew she'd have someone there at the table with us for our delayed Christmas dinner. The price of airline tickets dropped during the week after Christmas, so that's when I was traveling. Alex would return from his tropical Christmas, and we'd have one day to exchange gifts and celebrate Christmas before I left on my trans-Atlantic flight.

Well, we could exchange presents, if I found something to give him. I'd spent quite a few hours pondering what to buy for him. So far, I had zero options.

A faint female voice sounded through the phone line. Alex said, "Got to go. I'll call you later." We set a time to talk later, and I told myself there was no reason to feel down. Surely I wasn't one of those clingy women who couldn't enjoy themselves without a man on their arm. No, I'd never been like that. More often than not, I'd been alone and just fine with that. Missing someone was a new sensation, one that made me slightly uncomfortable. I wasn't at all sure that I wanted my happiness to be so dependent on another person's presence. With Alex living in the cottage just down the lane from mine and with both of us working on the same documentary series, we had slipped into an easy routine during the last few months, riding to work together and often having dinner or stopping to pick up groceries on the way home. It was all very domestic and cozy and...nice. To have him suddenly gone, left me feeling off-kilter. It was as if the last step on the stairs had suddenly disappeared. The expected was gone, and I was stumbling around as if I'd missed a step, trying to find my footing.

The last thing I wanted to do was mope around, contemplating the benefits and pitfalls of relationships, so I slipped on my black peacoat, wound my scarf around my neck, and took my temporary house guest,

Alex's greyhound, Slink, for a swift walk. Slink would have preferred a run, but I'm more of a walker than a runner, but she had a long leash and spent the time surging ahead, then loping back to me as if to say, *What's taking you so long?* I figured she covered twice the territory I did. Back at my cottage, she settled in for a long nap on her cushion, and I set out for the pub. Even though it was afternoon, I wanted a good cup of coffee.

The rain had stopped for the moment, but dark gray clouds seemed to hover only feet above the barren tree branches, darkening the afternoon so that it felt more like twilight. The little copse where the lane dead-ended was fuzzy and indistinct with mist. I tucked the umbrella under my arm and headed away from the copse toward the village, nodding as I passed a woman with short black hair who was emerging from a gray hatchback parked a few cottages down the lane. She looked startled and touched her black rectangular-framed glasses as if to see me better. She looked a bit familiar, but I couldn't place where I'd seen her. Probably somewhere around the village. Nether Woodsmoor was small enough that I saw the same people frequently, although it wasn't so small that I knew everyone's name.

The aptly named Cottage Lane was positioned on a rise slightly above the village of Nether Woodsmoor. And with no houses on the other side of the lane, I had an unimpeded view of the village, which was made up of cottages and shops constructed of mellow golden stone clustered around the village green and the sturdy church with its pointy spire, which today was shrouded in mist. The wide swiftly moving river cut through the village, reflecting the dark sky. Tiny white lights had been strung across the main thoroughfare, and the shops were decked out in lights, garlands, and bows. Even the street-lights had been wrapped in greenery. I cut down to the main road and joined the people on the sidewalk. With three days until Christmas, the shopping rush was on, even in tiny Nether Woodsmoor. I hurried on, the chilly damp air plenty of motivation to get to the pub quickly.

I stepped into the warmth of the White Duck Pub and made my way to the bar because all the tables around the crackling fire were filled. As I unwound my scarf and settled on a barstool, I caught sight of Louise's ponytail. Her black hair was often tinted a black-cherry color, but today her hair was an even more festive candy apple red. With her plump figure and protective manner, she had a motherly air, especially when she dealt with her employ-ees, but her bright, ever-changing hair color seemed to hint that she was a bit of a risk-taker. For some reason, I thought if she lived in the States, she'd own a Harley.

"Is it the usual today? Takeaway?" she asked.

"No, I'm off today."

She leaned back and blinked at me. "Off? You?"

"Oh, come on. I don't work that much...do I?"

Louise filled several pints and placed them on her tray. "Let's just say, when you stop in here you're either on your way to or from work." It was the sort of state-ment my mom had made frequently, which always set me on the defensive immediately, but I didn't have the same reaction to Louise. Her tone wasn't accusatory, merely factual. She was one of those people who had a knack for making you feel comfortable. With her unhurried manner, I felt as if she had all day to listen, a pretty good characteristic for a pub owner.

"I suppose that's true," I allowed. Being a location scout did fill most of the hours of my day. Maybe that's why I was a little blue. Going from a million miles an hour to…well…full stop was a bit disconcerting. Hours of uninterrupted peace and quiet to do whatever I wanted sounded lovely in the abstract. In reality, I felt adrift. "The production is shut down until after the New Year. Shopping is the only thing on my agenda. So I will have lunch, but not to-go."

Louise took my order for fish and chips as she lifted the tray. I pulled out my Moleskine notebook and studied the list of gifts I needed to purchase. I'd lined through every name on the list except for Alex's. I took out a pen and prepared to jot down a few ideas.

Louise returned with my food. "You've been frowning at that paper for a long while."

"I'm stumped. I have no idea what to get Alex for Christmas. He isn't into possessions, you know? I can't think of a single thing he really wants."

"What's that thing he used to do? Not skiing…" she asked.

"Snowboarding," I supplied as I picked up a crisp, or

what I thought of as a french fry. "But he's got all the gear for that, and he doesn't do it much now, anyway."

She nodded and rang up a check, then returned later to ask, "What about something for his camera?"

"I could get him a new lens or even a new camera, but that would be work-related. That seems…I don't know, not personal enough." I wiped my mouth with a napkin. "I want to get him something that strikes the right balance. Not anything too extravagant, but nothing too frivolous either. Nothing that puts the pressure on, but on the other hand, I want to show him how much I…appreciate him."

Louise's eyebrows, which were normally hidden behind her long bangs, lowered into view as she frowned. "That's a lot for one present to do, luv."

"I know. I've thought and thought and can't come up with anything. The days are ticking away. I have to get him *something*. At this point, I'll have to buy him a tie." I sighed. A tie would be the worst gift for Alex, who was laid-back and relaxed. His idea of dressing up was wearing khakis instead of jeans. "Or maybe a wallet."

Louise looked at me sympathetically, then tossed the dishrag she'd been holding into a bucket. "You should come with me," she said, decisively.

"Where?"

"To the Christmas Market in Upper Benning. Ella is here for the rest of the day. I have to finish my Christmas shopping. The market is huge. It's Regency-themed, too, so you can call it research."

"That could be interesting." At our last production meeting before we broke for the holiday, the producer of the documentary series, Elise DuPont, had said that when we reconvened in January, she wanted us to pitch her ideas for future episodes. "Dazzle me, people," she'd said.

The relationship between Elise and I had recently moved to a more solid footing after a shaky start, and a good pitch would keep everything positive between us. I wanted things to stay positive. I did not want to be on her naughty list again. A possible future Christmas-themed episode might be worth exploring. "And you think there will be a gift there that Alex would like? He's not that into the Regency stuff." He had read a few Austen novels because I recommend them, but he was far from a fanboy when it came to Jane Austen.

"The vendors dress in Regency costumes, but there are all sorts of stalls: food, crafts, artisan beer and wine, collectables. They have entertainment, the whole bit. And Harriet Hayden has a booth," she said in a tone that conveyed this fact should be the clincher for me.

"Who?"

"Harriet Hayden, the author. Surely, you've heard of her?"

"No."

"Oh, I can't believe you didn't know. And you, being such a big Jane Austen fan. In fact..." Louise bent and looked under the bar. "Yes, I thought Patricia said she'd finished it." Louise stood and held out a paperback book.

The cover showed a woman in a Regency walking dress and bonnet looking shyly up at a gentleman with an elaborate cravat, high collar points, and a well-fitted coat. A stately home filled the hazy distance in one corner of the cover while the title, *Lasting Impressions,* in an elaborate cursive font dominated the bottom third of the cover. I took the book from her and read the subtitle aloud, "A *Pride and Prejudice* Variation. What's that?"

"It means it takes place in the same world as Austen's *P & P*, but the story goes in a different direction than in Austen's book. It's a 'what if' scenario. You know, what if Elizabeth hadn't refused Darcy's first proposal, or what if her mother somehow forced her to become engaged to Mr. Collins? How would the story play out?"

"Oh, I get it. It's fan fiction." I flipped the book over and skimmed the list of titles by the author, which was quite long. "Your Harriet Hayden is prolific."

"We've read them all. The book club, I mean. My personal favorite is *Miss Bingley Suspects*. It's a spin-off, really, and starts a completely new series that has a lot of mystery in it as well as romance. Miss Bingley has to solve a murder at a house party and becomes quite a bit less stuffy in the process. Great fun." Louise pointed out the title, the first of six in the series then tapped another title. "If you like a sweet romance, you should read *To Ardently Love and Admire*. It's Mr. and Mrs. Gardiner's backstory. That's one of her best. The Page Turners loved it."

"Page Turners? Your book club?"

"Yes. You should come. We meet once a month and read something Austen-related, either one of Jane's books or something based on her work."

"I've never read any Jane Austen fan fiction," I said, thinking of Elise's demand that we amaze her with our pitches.

Louise had been leaning, elbows on the bar, but she straightened. "Anyway, Harriet Hayden is the main reason I'm going to the Christmas market. She's had a booth there the last few years. It's the only place to get an autographed copy of her latest book."

"She doesn't do book signings?"

"No." Louise frowned and shook her head. "I don't understand it. The chap at Slightly Foxed acts like he's never heard of her," Louise said, naming the only bookstore for miles around, which was located in Upper Benning. "The owner says he doesn't carry her books because she publishes them herself instead of through a big company." Louise shook her head. "It doesn't make sense to me. Harriet Hayden's new books are always best sellers. At least, online."

Nether Woodsmoor had plenty of tea shops, restaurants, and stores carrying quaint items that appealed to the weekend tourists who arrived in the area to bike and hike, but purchasing anything from books to housewares required either a trip to the next larger town, Upper Benning, or an online order.

Louise shrugged. "So, if I want an autographed copy of *Georgiana's Intrigue* it will have to be at the Christmas market. That's her latest. I already read it on my e-reader, but I like to have the autographed paper copy, too. Are you coming with me? It's just what you need to take your mind off this," she said with a nod at my Christmas list. "Come on, who knows what you'll find."

I closed the Moleskine notebook. "Sounds great. I'll run home and get Alex's car. He's letting me borrow it while he's gone."

Louise waved the idea away with an easy flick of her wrist. "Ride with me. My car's right here." She removed her green apron and greeted Ella, the teenager with long red hair who had stepped behind the bar.

I bundled up and followed Louise out of the pub. As we circled around to the back where her royal blue Ford Fiesta was parked, a movement along the street caught my eye. The road was busy with pedestrians toting shopping bags and compact cars zipping along, but my attention focused on one woman across the street, probably because she was staring at me. It was as if I could feel her gaze on me, which drew mine. It was the same woman I'd seen on Cottage Lane. She took a hesitant step forward, then stopped as a car tooted its horn at her. She stepped back on the curb as the car whisked by.

"Kate, are you coming?" Louise called from a few feet farther down the narrow alley that ran between the pub and another shop. "If you changed your mind and want to get your car, I'll wait. You can follow me."

I took a couple of steps down the alley. "No, that's fine." As I turned away, I got a last glimpse of the woman.

She stood, her face ambivalent as she watched me. Then she turned and got into the gray hatchback. I picked up my pace and joined Louise at her car. It almost seemed as if the woman was following me. But that was crazy. Why would anyone follow me?

CHAPTER 2

"WHAT'S WRONG, LUV?" LOUISE ASKED as she signaled to turn into the parking area reserved for the Christmas market.

I pulled my attention away from the side mirror. I couldn't think of a single reason anyone in the world would follow me, and I would have written off the two sightings of the woman as coincidence, except that she had been staring at me.

Both times.

I had watched the road behind us as Louise pulled out of her parking space behind the pub. A small gray hatchback had fallen in behind Louise's car before we crossed the bridge and left Nether Woodsmoor. The gloomy day made it hard to see the driver, but the hatchback never passed us or closed the distance. A few times, another car slipped in between us and the gray car, but eventually the other cars passed or turned off, revealing the headlights of the gray car still shining in the side view mirror.

"I saw a woman as we left the pub. She was outside my cottage earlier. Both times, she was watching me."

Louise gave me a worried look as she swung into a parking place.

"And I think she followed us here." I twisted around and looked out the back window, but no silver car cruised by. I opened my door and stepped out, scanning the parking area.

"It could have been just one of those things," Louise said. "Plenty of people out shopping today. Lots of silver cars, too."

"I suppose you're right." I picked up my purse. "On to the market," I said, trying to put some enthusiasm into my voice, but I continued to look at the cars as we walked to the green and its towering Christmas tree.

A petting zoo with several reindeer dominated one open area while a couple of stages ringed the tree. A country dance was in progress on one stage, the men and women lined up on opposite sides, stepping forward and back and weaving through the lines in elaborate patterns as music played over loudspeakers. We paused to watch the dancers, who were in Regency dress. I thought some of the women looked cold.

Bundled up children swarmed around a puppet show on another stage. Booths decorated with evergreen, twinkling lights, holly, and mistletoe ran around the perimeter of the green and spilled into some of the side streets, selling everything from evergreen wreaths to refrigerator magnets. The aroma of roasted chestnuts drifted our way from the food area, where I also spotted a tent serving hot chocolate and snacks. Most of the vendors were in traditional dress, the women's long skirts swishing as they moved and the men repeatedly lifting their chins as they tugged at their fancy cravats.

We browsed through the stalls, Louise picking up gifts for some of her employees, until I came to a stop in front of a booth selling antique prints. I saw one with a vintage car and flicked through the stack, stopping at a print ad with a red MG Midget convertible. The MG symbol floated in the background behind the images of the car. The text at the bottom of the ad touted the slogan, "Safety Fast!" It wasn't the same year model as Alex owned, but I knew he'd like it. I pulled it out and showed Louise. "I think Alex would like this."

"See, I knew you'd find something."

The owner stepped forward. "Sorry, but that one is sold." He pointed to a tiny sticker near the price tag. "I may have another one at my shop. Should I check for you?"

"Yes, please do," I said with a sigh. Of course the only potential gift I'd found was sold.

"I'll have to take your name and call you tomorrow." He reached for a pen and paper.

I gave him my phone number and found Louise outside the booth, consulting the free map of the booths that we'd picked up on our way in. "Where to now?" I asked. "Should we find your author?"

"Yes, she should be down this way, near the food." Louise strode briskly across the green. She stopped short outside a booth and read a sign aloud, "Harriet Hayden regrets that she is not able to be here." Louise's voice rose questioningly on the last words. "That can't be right."

Inside the booth, we stepped up to a table beside a haggard-looking woman with a half-grown out blond dye job that contrasted sharply with her own dark brown roots. I probably wouldn't have noticed her, except that once you entered the area around her, it was obvious that she hadn't showered in a few days. I shot a sideways glance at her and noticed she wasn't wearing a coat, only jeans and a worn brown sweatshirt that was fraying at the cuffs and neckline. She seemed quite different from most of the other attendees, who were bundled in thick coats and seemed to be mostly families with young kids or women shoppers intently working their way through the market. I wondered if the woman was homeless.

She stepped aside, making room for us at the table, which was set up with stacks of books, bookmarks, and an eight-by-ten photograph of a woman who looked to be in her mid-fifties with a round face, a generous smile, rosy cheeks, and shoulder-length pale brown hair parted on the side that hung straight to her shoulders. She exuded an air of quiet confidence as she smiled out from the photo.

Louise bent to read the smaller print on the sign. "See

All Things Jane for purchases." An arrow pointed to the right.

"But she *never* misses a Christmas market," Louise said. "Never. She's one of the original organizers."

"Exactly," said a voice directly behind me. Louise and I both turned. The scruffy woman was gone, but the woman I'd seen outside my cottage and the pub stood in front of me.

I stepped back instinctively. My legs bumped into the edge of the table and the photo toppled. The woman didn't look threatening, but I still wanted some distance between us. The way she'd quietly appeared directly behind me unnerved me. Up close, I could see that she was small-framed and petite. Her glasses were too heavy and clunky and overwhelmed her delicate bone structure.

"That's what I thought, too—" she broke off then smiled. "Louise! I didn't recognize you with your new hair color. I like it, very flattering with your porcelain skin. Here, let me fix this picture." She moved to the table.

"You know her?" I asked quietly to Louise while the woman's back was turned to us. "It's her, the woman who has been following me."

"Gina?" Louise said. "*Gina* has been following you? Why on earth?"

The woman adjusted the picture and turned back to us, looking embarrassed. "I do apologize, but I thought you might be able to help...about Harriet, you know.

Louise told us at the book club all about how you helped the police, and I thought, well, since the police don't seem to care, maybe you could look into it." Her hand fluttered up to her glasses. She repositioned them and said, "I'm sorry. I'm going about this completely the wrong way." She put out her hand. "I'm Gina Brill. I should have introduced myself this morning."

I shook her hand. "Kate Sharp. Nice to meet you." Now that she was talking in a soft, hesitant way, I didn't feel threatened.

"That's why I was outside your cottage," she continued, "but it seemed rather forward—walking straight up to you on your doorstep." She looked at Louise. "I should have had you ask her, Louise, but you're always so busy. I thought I'd do it myself, but…well," she turned back to me. "Once I saw you, it was as if everything I'd prepared to say just disappeared from my brain. I couldn't think of one word. So I followed you to the pub. I had just screwed up my courage to go in and talk to you when you left. So I followed you here."

"But why? I'm sorry, but I don't understand."

"Because of Harriet. Something is wrong. Very wrong. As Louise said, Harriet would never miss a Christmas market. I think," she faltered and repositioned her glasses before continuing, "I think something bad has happened to her. She wouldn't miss the Christmas market," Gina repeated then turned to Louise as she said, "And she was working on that Valentine novella, which she promised to let the book club read before she released it. She was very specific about the dates. She said she'd have it to us by December first and that she'd need it back from us by the New Year with feedback. She wouldn't forget something like that."

The draping that separated the booths was swept back on one side and a tall woman in a Regency bonnet and green velvet pelisse stepped into the booth. In contrast to her clothes, her narrow face was heavily made-up with thick eyeliner, false lashes, and pink lipstick. Her thick golden-brown hair hung down her back and heavy bangs stuck out from under the brim of the bonnet. "I thought I heard voices. Louise and Gina. Lovely to see you both. Stopping by for the latest Harriet Hayden book, are you? It's wonderful, as always." Despite her words, her dislike of the two women came across, even to me.

"Of course," Louise said, picking up a book off the top of a stack. "I never miss one."

"I know. You're lucky to get it. That's the last of the batch she signed before she left."

"Left for where?" Louise asked with a look out of the corner of her eye at Gina.

"The Canary Islands. She hadn't planned to be there over the holiday, but she called me and said it was so lovely that she just couldn't leave yet. Do you want to pick up anything else before I ring this up for you?" she asked.

"No, I have the rest," Louise said succinctly, and I realized that the dislike was mutual.

"Well, I want one." I reached for a copy of *Miss Bingley Suspects*. "I've heard this one is really good." I smiled at Louise.

Gina said, "Oh, yes. One of my favorites. She's at the top of her game in that one."

The woman cut her glance toward Gina sharply. "Harriet Hayden is always at the top of her game." Then she turned to me and extended her hand. "Always a pleasure to meet another Janeite. I'm Carrie Webbington. Maybe you'd like to take a look around my booth before I ring this up?"

"Um…sure. I'm Kate," I said as we followed her through the gap in the draping. Every square inch in Carrie's booth was filled with tables and portable shelves displaying anything and everything with either a Jane Austen quote or an Austen profile, including mugs and tea sets, shawls and jewelry, keychains and phone covers, tote bags and note cards, even boy short panties with Austen quotes. It was overwhelming. She had to be going for festive and Christmassy, but all of it together added up to claustrophobic. "No, just the book for now. I may be back later."

"Excellent," Carrie said as she handed Louise a bag with the words *All Things Jane* printed on it in a hypercurly font over a silhouette of Austen.

Louise moved outside the booth to wait with Gina for me. Inside the booth, a tense silence descended as Carrie rang up my book.

To break the atmosphere, I said, "You mentioned the author is in the Canary Islands. My boyfriend is there."

"What a *coincidence*," Carrie said, seizing the topic. "It is a wonderful place, I hear, so I guess it's not that surprising. It's a very popular destination, particularly at this time of year with the cold weather here. Harriet says it's absolutely amazing. We're neighbors, you know, Harriet and I. We're very close. Harriet says it's like a tropical dream there." She handed me a plastic bag and wiggled her fingers at Louise and Gina.

"Tropical dream, my foot," Gina said as soon as I'd joined them, and we'd walked a few steps away. The music for another dance began. A vendor called out to us, trying to get us to try his fish and chips. Gina glanced back over her shoulder at the booth, then lowered her voice, despite the racket going on around us. "Harriet loves Christmas and this market. She'd never choose to spend her Christmas anywhere but in England."

"So you think she's what? In trouble?" I asked.

"Worse. I think..." Gina's voice trailed off. She looked over to the Christmas tree, her face sad. She drew in a steadying breath and fixed her glasses firmly on her nose. "I think she's dead."

CHAPTER 3

I EXCHANGED A GLANCE WITH Louise. Gina's words were stunning, but she looked so distraught that I thought she really meant them.

Louise looked at her friend with concern. "Let's get a cup of cocoa and sit down."

I offered to get the drinks and went to turn in our order, hot chocolate for me and Louise—it seemed like a hot chocolate kind of day—and peppermint tea for Gina. "We'll have it out in a moment," said a young girl in a Santa hat.

I turned around and nearly bumped into the person in line behind me. I apologized and stepped around her, realizing it was the rather smelly woman from Harriet Hayden's booth. I found Louise and Gina seated at one end of a deserted table and slid into the long bench opposite them.

Louise nodded at Gina and said, "Tell us all about it, why don't you?"

Gina blew out a breath. "It sounds so...absurd when I say it aloud. That's why I hesitated to approach you, Kate. But I really do think that something awful has happened to Harriet." Gina shifted so that she faced me directly. "I work at the grocery, you see. That's how I met Harriet. She came in at least once a week to do her shopping. I always chat with the customers, and I got to know her a little bit. Then I found out she was *the* Harriet Hayden. I should have made the connection on my own, of course. I saw her name when she used her card, but it never even crossed my mind that she could be one of my favorite authors. Her picture isn't in the back of her book, you see. And you don't expect to meet people like that in your everyday life, do you? One of the librarians pointed her out to me at a library event. I was never so surprised." Gina paused as the server arrived, the same teen girl in the Santa hat. She handed out steaming mugs.

Gina took a sip of her tea before continuing, "Now you might think that I didn't know Harriet Hayden that well, but you'd be surprised at what you learn about someone while working at the grocery." Gina shot a glance at Louise, who nodded.

"I believe you," Louise said. "I know all kinds of things that people don't want to broadcast, and I'm not even seeing what they have in their trolleys."

Gina sipped and nodded. "Yes. I know who bought a pregnancy test last week and which gentleman is suddenly not living at home, from the amount of ready meals he's suddenly picking up."

I got that weird feeling that someone was watching me. I glanced around and made eye contact with the haggard woman with the bad dye job. She was seated behind us at another table and had both red-chapped hands wrapped around her mug. When our gaze met, she looked away and took a sip from her mug.

Gina leaned toward me, drawing me back into the conversation. "It's not that I *want* to know these things, but there they are. I can't help seeing them or that I have a good memory."

"So did Harriet Hayden have some sort of secret that you discovered?" I asked.

"Oh, no," Gina said, her tone scandalized that I'd even suggest it. "No, it was nothing like that. I just want you to know that even though she wasn't my close friend, I knew her. She came in regular as clockwork, Tuesdays, three-thirty. Her break time, she called it. She wrote every weekday and weekends when she was on a deadline. She does go on holiday, but only for a week or two at a time, to visit friends or, a few times, on longer trips. She went to Portugal once and Italy another time, but she always came home after a week or so. She never stayed gone months at a time. Christmas was her favorite time of year. That's one of the reasons she put so much effort into getting this market off the ground. She knew it would be a success. I know she wouldn't miss it. She wouldn't. She's been gone since November," Gina said, touching the table with her forefinger to emphasize the point. "She would not willingly miss the Christmas market."

"I'm sorry that you're worried about your friend, and it does sound rather...odd." I picked my words carefully because I didn't want to hurt Gina's feelings. "But why would you want to talk to me about this? If you're worried about her, you should talk to the police."

She jerked her head in an impatient gesture. "The police. I've talked to them, and they won't listen."

"Why not?"

"Because they contacted someone in the Canary Islands and got back word that Harriet is fine," she said, her tone scornful. "Just because the hotel manager says she's there, doesn't mean she is. People can be bribed, you know. If she's there, why won't she answer her calls?"

From the little I'd seen of her, Gina seemed to be a mostly reserved person with a soft voice and a hesitant manner. She didn't seem to be the type who got worked up often, but she was agitated now. She took a breath, then sipped her tea, taking a moment, and then she continued in a more reasonable tone. "That's why I need you. Louise told me all about your work with the police. You can find out what happened to Harriet. You can catch her killer."

I blinked. It took me a few moments to actually form a sentence. "Saying that I worked with the police is stretching it. I'm flattered you think I could help, but I'm afraid I'd be useless to you. I was only able to help those other times because I knew the people involved and had sort of an inside track. Special knowledge of the situation, I guess you'd say. I'm not connected to anyone you've mentioned. I'd be completely clueless here."

"Oh, but I already know who did it. I just need you to help me figure out how to prove it. Louise says you're very clever."

I'd been about to take a drink of my watery hot chocolate, but put the mug down. "You know that Harriet is dead *and* who killed her?" I asked as I looked toward Louise. Was Gina really a stable person? She appeared to be, but normally people didn't go around talking about knowing a killer's identity so blithely.

"It was Carrie Webbington, of course," Gina said.

"The woman whose shop we were just in?" I asked, checking Louise's reaction to Gina's announcement.

Louise set down her hot chocolate, then raised her hands and leaned back in a don't-ask-me posture. "I don't like the woman, myself, so I'm not a good judge. She certainly seems like someone who could bump off another human being without a second thought."

"She thought long and hard about it, I'm sure," Gina said. "She had motive and opportunity." Gina ticked each item off on her fingers. "She lives in the semi beside Harriet. So she was right there with her. Plenty of opportunity."

"Semi? I don't know what that is," I said.

Louise said, "Semi-detatched. Two houses that are joined with a common wall."

"Oh, like a duplex," I said, nodding.

"And Carrie has always been greedy." Gina paused to pat Louise's arm. "I'm sorry to bring it up, but it's true. And it's pertinent."

Louise made a face. "No worries. I got over Randy a long time ago." Louise looked at me. "Carrie and I go way back. Before I moved to Nether Woodsmoor, she and I worked at the same restaurant in Manchester. She stole my guy." Louise shrugged. "Water under the bridge."

"But still, it's a pattern," Gina said firmly. "She wants more than she has—that's motive. She's not a true Janeite either. She only sells those things because they're profitable. I saw her online store when she first opened. She had all sorts of tacky things. Only the Jane Austen merchandise sold, so she stuck with that. You saw how she's taken over Harriet's booth and is selling her books. You can't tell me that the royalties off Harriet's books wouldn't be worth killing for. Her books are best sellers."

"Only online though," Louise cautioned.

Gina took another sip of her tea, grimaced, and put it down. "I did some research over the last few days. Her books may sell mostly online, but she's made the *New York Times* list three separate times as well as several other lists. Her books sell. She has to be making good money, and Carrie is transferring it into her account, I'm sure, or simply withdrawing it in cash."

"That should be easy enough to check. You've told all this to the police?" I asked.

"No, they won't talk to me." She took another sip of her tea, then set it aside with a shudder. "That's awful. I don't know what they put in it. I should have had the cocoa," she murmured, then looked down at her folded hands. "I'm afraid I've been banned from my local constabulary," she said primly.

"Surely not," Louise said.

"Well, not officially, but Constable Petrie won't speak to me on the subject any more. He holds up his hand and shakes his head when I try to talk to him now. He says they checked, and Harriet is fine, so I have to leave it alone. But I *can't*. Not when I know something terrible has happened."

"I'm sorry, but I don't think—"

She reached across the table and took my hand. Her hand was very cold. "Please," she said with a beseeching gaze that rivaled the pitiful look Slink sent me when she wanted a walk. "At least let me tell you what I've found out before you say no."

I sighed. I couldn't resist her sad gaze. And she was so insistent. "All right," I said, "but I don't think I'll be able to help you."

"That's fine, just talking through it may jog my memory, or you might notice something I missed." She shifted around on the bench and reached for her handbag, but stopped abruptly and put her hand to her forehead. "Oh, a bit of a head rush there." She carefully moved so that she wasn't twisted around. "Sorry. I'm okay now." She put a pocket-size spiral notebook with a red cover on the table and flipped to a page that was folded down at the corner.

She blinked and held the notebook at arm's length, seeming to struggle to focus on the page. After a second, she handed it to me with a shake of her head. "My eyes are tired. It's all there. I don't need to read it. I've looked at it so many times I have it memorized. The last time I saw Harriet at the grocery was in November. It was a Tuesday, her usual shopping time. She didn't buy as much as she normally did because she was leaving for a trip to the Canary Islands, the day after she came to Page Turners. That's our book club," Gina explained.

"Yes. Louise told me. Was Harriet a member, too?"

"Oh, no," Gina said. "We invited her to talk about her books. We were thrilled that she could do it. So nice of her to make time, right before her trip, but that was Harriet all over. Thoughtful, you know, despite being so busy. It was such a fun night. We met at the White Duck, of course, and had a wonderful time. So interesting to hear about her process. She writes a twenty-page outline in longhand, then when she's writing, she saves all her work to one of those small memory devices. What did she call it? Oh yes, a flash drive. Keeps it with her all the time," Gina said.

Louise nodded. "She doesn't like 'the cloud.' She said she lost power and her Internet connection once when she was on a tight deadline and couldn't get to her book."

"Anyway, the last time I spoke to her was the third Friday in November, after the book club," Gina said.

Louise wrapped both hands around her mug of hot chocolate. "Yes, we all walked out together that night. Gina and Harriet stayed while I closed up."

"She said she was leaving the next day for her trip, and she would return a week later on Saturday, November twenty-eighth. We talked about the Christmas market and how much she was looking forward to it."

Gina paused, her gaze focused on the green and white tablecloth. "I'm sorry to say that I didn't realize she wasn't back until December. It was the change of the month, you know, that jogged my memory. I thought, *oh, I will ask Harriet about her trip when she comes in this week*. But she didn't. I thought I'd missed her. But when the second week of December went by, and no one had seen her at the grocery, I went by her house. It was shut up tight. Blinds closed, and the little step covered with dead leaves. Carrie came up the walk at that moment, a key in her hand, as bold as brass. She *said* she was bringing in the mail for Harriet, that Harriet had called and said she extended her trip, and would Carrie get the mail for her? I didn't believe her for a moment." Gina put her hand on her stomach and swallowed determinedly.

"Are you okay?" I asked. Gina's skin had a washed out look to it, and I noticed her forehead was suddenly shiny. If talking about her friend brought on this physical reaction, she really was worried about Harriet.

Gina gripped the edge of the table, wrinkling the paper cloth as she drew in an unsteady breath. "No, I'm afraid I'm going to be ill." She turned and half-crawled along the long bench, then stumbled away, weaving along the side of the tented dining area. Louise shifted along the bench, following her. I stood and stepped over the bench then hurried around the end of the table to Gina. She'd stopped and was doubled over in pain, her hands clutched at her midsection.

"Someone call for help," I said as I put a hand on her back.

"No—need...air." She pushed herself upright and with her hands braced on one of the tables she took a few steps, faltered, and fell, her head cracking against the edge of the table as she collapsed.

CHAPTER 4

A WHITE-COATED MAN WITH thinning hair and round glasses opened the door to the waiting room and consulted a file. "Louise Clement?"

The attention of the people scattered around the brightly lit room dropped away as they shifted back into the vinyl chairs. Louise and I stood as the man walked over.

"I'm Doctor Hardy. You're a friend of," he paused to check the file again, "Mrs. Brill?"

"Ms. Brill," Louise corrected. "She's not married."

"Any children or other family?" the man asked.

"As I told them at admission, no. Her nearest relative is a cousin in Canada." Louise's voice was impatient. "How is she?"

He made a note in the file, then put his pen away as he looked at Louise over the rims of his glasses, which had slipped down his nose. He sighed. "I really shouldn't—"

"Dr. Hardy," Louise said in a firm tone that I'd never heard her use. "Even if I could get in touch with Gina's cousin, it would take her at least a day or more to get here. I am one of Gina's closest friends. How is she? What happened?"

"That's my question for you. You said she fell, then complained of nausea?"

"No, that's completely wrong." Louise pushed her red bangs out of her eyes with an impatient gesture. "She said she was going to be sick then wrapped her arms around her stomach. She was clearly in pain. Then she fell and hit her head. We couldn't wake her."

The doctor's attitude changed from briskly businesslike to intense concentration. "She didn't fall first?"

"No, that's what I just said—what we've told everyone from the emergency people who arrived at the market to the admissions people," Louise said, her voice testy.

"She said she felt dizzy, too," I added, "and she looked very pale."

Dr. Hardy ignored Louise's irate tone. "And she had ingested tea?" he asked.

"Yes, peppermint tea, at the Christmas market. Again, how is she? I'd like to see her."

Dr. Hardy had already moved backwards a few steps as Louise asked her question. "We're doing everything we can," he said. "I'll update you soon." He turned and jogged away, disappearing through the doors.

Louise sagged into the nearest chair. "Really. Doesn't

anyone listen? I told them—all of them—exactly what happened."

I did my best to soothe Louise, but the doctor's quick exit worried me. I settled in to wait, expecting it to be a long time before anyone came with more news, but less than twenty minutes later Dr. Hardy pushed through the doors again. Louise had been trying to find someone who could get in touch with Gina's Canadian cousin, and I had been paging through Gina's notebook. She'd left it with me when she left the table. In the commotion after she fell, I'd tucked it in my coat pocket. I had been skimming over her notes, but it was hard to concentrate with the activity in the waiting room—people moving through the chairs, making calls, and one baby who wasn't at all happy.

"No, don't get up." Dr. Hardy sat down beside Louise. "Your friend is still in critical condition and unconscious. You can't see her now, but it may be possible tomorrow. I expect her to improve, now that the poison is out of her system."

"Poison?" Louise said. "What are you talking about?"

"Ms. Brill ingested between ten and fifteen mistletoe berries."

"But she didn't have anything but the tea..." Louise's voice trailed off, and I felt a little nauseous myself.

Dr. Hardy asked, "Did anyone save her cup?"

Louise seemed to be lost in her own thoughts and didn't answer, so I said, "No. We didn't know...I mean, I could tell she was sick, but it never occurred to me to think it might have something to do with the tea."

Louise put out a hand and touched my arm. "She said it tasted funny, remember? When she was almost done with it."

"Yes, she did," I said. "But she'll be okay now?"

"I'm actually more worried about the blow to the head than the poison. She has a concussion and some swelling. Medically speaking, mistletoe poisoning is the lesser of the two worries. Every holiday season the warnings about mistletoe are made, but overall, very few cases of mistletoe poisoning are fatal. Most people recover after some gastric distress. The head wound is what we'll keep an eye on. We should know more tomorrow. But, of course the poison does matter to the police," Dr. Hardy continued. "We've contacted them. Standard procedure. They'll sort it out. I'm sure they'll want to speak to you. Ah, there he is now. If you'll excuse me?"

Dr. Hardy left to meet a uniformed police officer who had entered the waiting room.

Louise looked down at Gina's notebook, which I had dropped into my lap. "Do you think..."

"It must be," I said. "Gina must be right. Why else would someone try to poison her?"

Constable Petrie didn't share our opinion.

At the mention of Gina's name, he quirked his mouth into a disapproving line. "At it again, is she?"

Dr. Hardy, who had just brought the constable over to Louise and me, said, "You can get in touch with me here, if you need additional information," and strode rapidly away.

Constable Petrie was probably in his late twenties, I guessed. He had a prominent brow with thick eyebrows that nearly met over close-set eyes and a pointed chin, which gave his face a triangular shape.

He took Louise and me around a corner into another waiting room and printed all our contact details into his notebook, then listened to us recount what happened, but there was an air of barely-suppressed impatience about him. Louise still seemed stunned by the news about the poison, so I'd taken the lead in detailing what had happened at the Christmas market and finished by saying, "Neither one of us had any idea. We didn't realize until Dr. Hardy told us about the mistletoe."

"And was anyone else with you at the table?" Petrie rubbed his hand along his pointy chin.

"No, just the three of us," I said. "Gina is worried about a friend of hers." I paused, trying to think of how to phrase things so that he'd listen. It seemed a bit extreme to mention the word *murder* at this point, especially since Gina had said the police had been dismissive of her worries about Harriet. "Gina's worried that her friend is hurt or possibly in trouble—"

"Harriet Hayden," Petrie said, cutting me off. "Right. Know all about it."

I held out Gina's notebook. "These are her notes."

Petrie flipped through the first pages, then handed it back. "I don't need this." He closed his own notebook and stood, obviously preparing to leave.

"You don't want her notes? Someone tried to poison her," I said, still holding the notebook out toward him.

"I have all that. Ms. Brill sends me *weekly updates.*" He made air quotes around the last two words. "As if she's running some sort of investigation. She's a woman with too much time on her hands, who has become a little too fixated on a semi-famous person."

"You don't think there's anything suspicious about Harriet Hayden's extended absence?" I asked.

"What absence? She's in a hotel in the Canary Islands. She extended her holiday. No crime in that."

Louise, who had been very quiet, leaned forward suddenly. "You're not taking Gina's poisoning seriously."

Petrie tapped his notebook. "I took down everything you said. We'll look into it, but I wouldn't be a bit surprised if Ms. Brill did it to herself. I'm sure the doctor gave you the same news he gave me. Mistletoe doesn't kill people, only makes them sick. This whole thing," he circled his notebook indicating the hospital walls, "could be an attempt to get us to check into the Hayden thing again."

"But what if Gina's right? What if someone did

murder Harriet Hayden?" Louise asked. "If Gina figured it out, then she'd be a target, too."

Petrie sighed and repeated his words slowly as if he were talking to a small child. "Hayden hasn't been murdered. She's on holiday." He stood and said, "Thank you for your time. We'll be in touch if we need more information."

We watched him until he turned the corner of the hallway. "Someone poisoned Gina, and the police don't care one bit," Louise said, amazement in her tone. "He's not going to do anything."

I blew out a long breath. I hadn't pictured spending the days before Christmas this way, but when I thought of Gina's horrible pale face and the pain that had wracked her body I knew there was only one thing to say. "But we can."

CHAPTER 5

"I'M IN," LOUISE SAID AS we exited the hospital, and the cold air engulfed us. "Of course, I'll do whatever I can to help. Someone has to do *something*, but I have no idea what it is that we should do."

I turned up the collar of my coat against the stiff wind that had sprung up. It had swept the clouds away, revealing a starry sky. "I suppose we have to do two things. First, we need to find out if Harriet really is in the Canary Islands. If she's there—and happy—well, then that eliminates Gina's suspicions about Carrie Webbington. Second, we need to find out if there is a reason someone other than Carrie would try to hurt Gina."

Louise unlocked the car doors. We had followed the ambulance from the market to the hospital. "But who would want to do that? I know Gina scared you today, skulking around after you, but that's only because she's rather timid. She doesn't have any enemies."

"It sounds as if she's well on the way to making an enemy out of Carrie Webbington."

Louise waved her hand. "No one likes Carrie. She's one of those personalities...what do they call them on the telly? Caustic? No, toxic. That's it. She contaminates and damages everyone she comes in contact with. She's the exception that proves the rule. Everyone else loves Gina."

"But Gina did say that she knew a lot of secrets from her job. Maybe someone felt threatened by her."

Louise slammed her door with more force than was necessary and sent me a disappointed look. "You don't know Gina the way I do. She wouldn't...I don't know... hold anything over someone's head."

"I'm not saying that she did. But maybe someone *thought* she was a threat. Maybe Gina knew something that could be very damaging to someone, either their reputation or their livelihood or...I don't know something else."

Louise started the car, her face set. "No, you heard her today. Being pregnant or having marriage problems is no reason to try to poison someone."

"Not normally, but someone did put poison in her tea. We should check it out, just to be thorough. We don't want to be like Constable Petrie, someone who already has his mind made up."

Louise's posture relaxed a bit. She looked at me out of the corner of her eye and cracked a small smile. "Comparing me to Petrie, eh? That's low. But effective. He's like a horse with blinders, and I don't want to be like that. Right. So I guess I'm talking to Gina's friends at work."

"Do you know anyone there?"

"Yes. Shondra Rashid works with her and is part of the book club. I'll start with her." Louise checked the dashboard clock. "Ella opens the pub tomorrow, so I can go back to Upper Benning in the morning."

"Okay," I said, flipping through the pages of Gina's notebook, which I had put in my pocket when Constable Petrie refused it. "Let's see if Gina knew where Harriet was staying. Here it is. The Royal Palm Resort. I'll ask Alex if he can check there for Harriet."

"HARRIET HAYDEN WASN'T at the Royal Palm Resort today," Alex said when he called me the next afternoon.

"Really?" I'd filled Alex in on what had happened last night as soon as I arrived back at my cottage. He had agreed to drop by the Royal Palm Resort. "Any excuse for a break from the family togetherness is a good excuse," he'd said.

I'd spent the morning on the Internet, looking for evidence that Harriet had been online recently. She had active accounts on all the big social media sites, which featured her and her books, but none of the accounts had been updated within the last few weeks. I checked the feeds, browsing backward in time, and discovered that the gaps in posts weren't that unusual for Harriet. She often went several weeks, sometimes a month or more without posting. Then she would put up a message, something along the lines of, "Out of the writing cave. Book is done!" In mid-November, she had posted a flurry of updates about looking forward to her upcoming trip, then nothing.

Alex continued, "The front desk wouldn't confirm that she's a guest, but the bartender knew her. He said Harriet mentioned returning home to England soon, but she also wanted to visit La Gomera before she left. That's another one of the islands."

I smiled, knowing that if the front desk wouldn't answer his questions, Alex would have used some of his location scouting techniques, which often involved an end run around red tape, to get answers. "So the bartender has seen her?"

"Yes, said she'd been in for drinks almost every night for the last three or four weeks. I figure she's either island hopping for the day, or she's checked out, and the resort doesn't want to give out info on their guests."

"Well, that's a relief. So the police were right." I told him about my morning online. "I was beginning to think that Gina might be right about Harriet because she certainly hasn't been posting updates about her trip on her Facebook newsfeed."

"Maybe she's been writing," Alex said.

"I hope so."

"I'm heading back to the resort to see if I can spot Harriet myself. Happy hour is only a few hours away."

"Do you have time for that?"

"Sure," he said easily. "Any word from Louise?"

"She called me earlier today. Gina is still in the hospital. No change in her condition. Louise spoke to Gina's coworker at the market. She says that the only customer Gina was especially interested in was Harriet. In fact, Gina was so serious about her search that she missed work a couple of times. Her friend covered for her."

"How, um, stable is this Gina?" Alex asked.

"I've been asking myself that question since yesterday. When she wasn't sneaking around following me, she seemed fine. I got the impression that she's usually pretty timid, but this thing with Harriet, well, she's very adamant about it."

"Sounds a bit...obsessive."

"I know." I sighed. "But she's in the hospital after being poisoned."

Alex said, "Hopefully, I'll run Harriet to ground tonight. If she's still here, I'll try to convince her to get in touch with Gina."

"Thank you for doing this, Alex. I appreciate you taking time out of your holiday for it."

"Don't worry about it. I'm taking my camera. I don't have to look very hard to find some views that demand a commercial or print ad be shot in them."

“It would be just awful if we had to return there for work.”

“Terrible.” I could hear the smile in his tone. “What are you doing now?”

“Sitting in your car on the street outside Harriet’s house. I’d hoped to talk to some of the neighbors, see if anyone had seen her, but no one was home. I figured I could stick around a few hours, that someone might come home for lunch, but no luck.” While location scouting, I’d spent many hours waiting for homeowners so that I could make my pitch in person. Sitting for a few hours in a car with *Miss Bingley Suspects* propped up on the steering wheel was no hardship. “I brought my camera, too, but this street won’t work for anything historical. Too many light poles and wires.” I carried my camera with me almost everywhere. It was second nature to pick it up on my way out the door along with my purse. It was something that my first boss in the location scouting business had drummed into me: *Always bring your camera.*

“Tropics, it is then. Glad that’s settled. I should go. The cell phone service isn’t good at the resort. It may be tonight before I can let you know what happened.”

“That’s fine. Talk to you then.”

His voice softened. “Hey, avoid peppermint tea for a few days, okay?”

“Of course. You know me. Coffee or nothing. Well, most of the time. I did have hot chocolate the other day, but coffee is usually my first choice,” I said, thinking how glad I was that when I decided to deviate from my usual drink choice that I'd picked hot chocolate and not tea.

I hung up and saw I had a voicemail. I listened to it as I tucked a bookmark into my book. It was the owner of the booth with the prints. "I didn't have another of the MG prints myself," he said, and my heart sank. That meant the search for a gift was back on. "But," he continued, "I have found one that I can order for you." He reeled off his phone number. I called him back and told him yes, I wanted it.

"Righto," he said. "I'll see if I can get it delivered. You do want it before Christmas?"

"Yes, definitely," I said, then hung up and gave the neighborhood a final scan as I reached for the ignition. A flutter of movement at one of the windows on Harriet's side of the house caught my eye. I released the ignition and watched the house. A few seconds later, I again saw a shadow move through one of the front rooms.

Perhaps Harriet had returned home? Maybe Alex had just missed her. If she'd left the resort yesterday or even this morning, she could be home by now. And even though I hadn't seen anyone approach the house, she might have a back entrance like the one at my cottage. If I was returning home from certain parts of the village, I often took the shorter path that ran behind my cottage and entered that way. Perhaps Harriet had done that. Or maybe she'd been home for hours. Small garages bracketed each side of the larger home. The garage on Harriet's side of the house was closed, but her car might already be in there.

I pocketed the car keys and climbed out of the car, kicking myself for skipping Harriet's house when I knocked on all the doors in the neighborhood. Instead of a small yard or garden, the area in front of both her house and Carrie's was covered with brick pavers. It was a newer home than most of the ones in Nether Woodsmoor, which were built of stone. This one was made of stucco, but it had a completely different look than the Mediterranean-style stucco homes that I was so familiar with in Southern California. These were designed in the cottage style, but this area had a definite suburban feel to it. The doors of both houses were set side-by-side in the center of the building. I reached out to ring the bell of the door on the left, but before I could push the button, the door swung open.

A woman stopped short in the doorway. Clearly, she was leaving and hadn't expected to find me on the doorstep. It wasn't Harriet. "I'm sorry," I began, thinking I must have mixed up the address that Louise had given me. I took a step back then stopped. "Wait. You're the woman from the Christmas market," I said, recognizing dark roots at the crown of her head and the blond ends of her hair that brushed her gaunt cheekbones. Behind her, on the wall of the narrow hallway, I saw several framed book covers with curly fonts and images of women in Regency clothes. "This *is* Harriet's house. Is she home?"

The woman scanned the street behind me, then she gripped my wrist and yanked me over the threshold. I jerked my arm away, but she was quicker than I was and had the door closed before I could get back outside. With her bony hand splayed on the door to keep it firmly closed, she said, "What do you know about Harriet? Where is she?"

CHAPTER 6

"I DON'T KNOW WHERE HARRIET is." My heart raced, but I tried to make my voice calm. The scruffy woman looked nervous enough for both of us. Her gaze skittered around the room, and her breathing was shallow and fast. The sweaty, unwashed smell was still strong. "That's what I asked you," I said. "Do you know where she is?"

"No. She should be here. She's always here."

"Are you a friend of hers?" I glanced around, looking for a way out through the back of the house.

The woman made a little noise that was halfway between a laugh and a snort. "No, I'm her sister." She removed her hand from the door and extended it. "Bridgette Hayden, black sheep of the family."

"Kate Sharp." Her hand was bony, all jutting knuckles, but the strength of her grip surprised me. Despite the woman's thin face, I could see a bit of resemblance to the photo I'd seen of Harriet. They both had the same generous mouth and natural flush in their cheeks, but Harriet had looked happy and confident. This woman was skittish and worried.

"I've never met Harriet," I said. "A friend of mine is worried about her, though."

"The mousey one with the dark hair that they took away in the ambulance last night?" Bridgette asked.

"Yes."

Bridgette pushed her stringy hair off her face. "I'm worried about Harriet, too. I heard your group mention Harriet's name in her booth, so I tagged along, hoping to hear more. Kitchen's this way. Should be some tea." She turned and walked away.

The anxious look on her face was the reason I didn't leave at that moment. I'd been in plenty of uncomfortable situations in stranger's homes when I scouted for locations. If I got a weird feeling, or felt scared, I got out right away, but I wasn't getting those vibes here. "None for me," I said quickly. Then added, "Thanks, though." I wasn't about to accept tea from anyone, least of all a stranger who had been near us at the time Gina was poisoned.

"American, right?" Bridgette said as I followed her through a sparsely-furnished living area to a kitchen with white cabinets and sleek stainless appliances. A sunroom, which was used as an office, extended into the back garden. A desk with a laptop and printer were positioned facing the back garden. Book-lined shelves filled the area under the expanse of windows, and a deep leather chair and ottoman were set off to the side, the perfect reading nook.

Bridgette had been opening cabinet doors while I looked around. She held up a teapot. "You sure? I'm having some."

"Thanks, but no."

"Suit yourself."

I wrapped my arms around my waist. It was very cool in the house. Harriet had probably turned down the heat when she left for her trip. Bridgette, who was still in the same threadbare sweatshirt and jeans from yesterday, didn't seem to notice. She rummaged around in the cabinets some more as she said, "This isn't like Harriet at all. To do a bunk. That's more my line." Bridgette put a box of crackers on the bar that separated the kitchen from the sunroom and gestured for me to sit at one of the barstools.

I took a seat but waved off the crackers. "Harriet told Gina that she was going to the Canary Islands back in November."

Standing on the other side of the counter, Bridgette had already consumed three of the thin crackers, but she paused. "That's what? Three, four weeks ago?" She shook her head. "Harriet wouldn't be gone that long, not without telling me. We don't get along, but she keeps in touch." She ate a few more crackers, then went to get the teapot, which had begun to whistle. "She doesn't agree with some of my 'lifestyle choices,' as she calls them." She closed her eyes briefly. "She sounds just like mum when she says that."

Bridgette sat down beside me and heaved a massive sigh, making me think of Slink when she settled down into her cushion after a long sprint. "But Harriet is right." Bridgette pulled a face. "She always is. Very annoying. Makes being her baby sister quite a challenge. Too much to live up to. That's what my shrink at the center told me, anyway." She chewed a moment. "I think it's true.

"Harriet always told me that when I was ready to get my life straightened out, she'd help me." She plucked at her sweatshirt and waved a hand at her greasy hair. "So here I am, looking like a war refugee, ready to admit that she's right. I lost my flat, but I'm twenty-two days clean." She pushed the cracker crumbs into a pile. "I can't do it. Not on my own. She's right. I need some help." Her gaze went glassy. "I need Harriet."

A pounding at the front door made both of us jump. "Police, open up."

Bridgette, eyes wide, stood and knocked over her barstool as she bolted out the back door. The last I saw of her was her skinny legs as they slithered over a wooden fence that enclosed the back garden.

It took about an hour to convince the police I hadn't broken into Harriet's house.

I shifted on Harriet's oatmeal-colored sofa and said, "I

don't know where Bridgette went. We only talked for a few minutes."

The policeman scratched his forehead, pushing his cap up a bit. "Odd, that you'd come inside and chat with a woman you didn't know."

"She said she was Harriet's sister. I hoped she knew where Harriet was."

The officer looked down at his notes. "You said you saw this woman earlier?"

He wasn't interested in Harriet. I'd tried to tell him about her, but he only wanted to talk about Bridgette. The front door opened, and another officer said, "We got the runner. Found her three blocks over at a bus shelter."

I breathed a little easier as the first officer left to talk to his colleague. Bridgette could confirm what I told them. At least, I hoped she would back up my story.

"But they are there illegally. I *insist* you arrest them." The officer had left the front door partly open, but I was sure I would have been able to hear the shrill voice through a closed door. I could see Carrie Webbington out the front window. She stood on the sweep of brick pavers in front of her house and jabbed her finger at Harriet's front door. "I heard them. The walls are very thin. I always knew when Harriet was home," she said loudly. "And she's not home. They're intruders."

My phone, which was in my coat pocket, rang. Alex's name was on the display.

"So glad you called," I said. "You'll come home and

bail me out, right? You do have bail in the U.K., don't you?"

"What?"

I told him what had happened then said, "So right now, I'm waiting for the officer to come back. I hope, I *really* hope, that Bridgette backs up what I said. Oh, wait, here he comes. I'll call you back." I slipped the phone into my pocket.

"You can leave as long as you're returning to Nether Woodsmoor. We'll be in touch, Ms. Sharp. We may need to follow up with you."

So Bridgette had come through for me. The officer disappeared back into the kitchen, before I could ask any more questions. I didn't linger. I slipped out the front door, and avoided looking Carrie's way. She was turned slightly away from me, and I scooted across the brick paved area, skirting around two officers who were talking to Bridgette.

"I've done nothing wrong," Bridgette said. "My sister gave me a key. She didn't mind if I dropped by. Here, look at my keys. That one is Harriet's. She gave it to me."

I wasn't sure about that statement about dropping in. It sounded as if the relationship between Harriet and Bridgette was complex and possibly strained, but the two officers exchanged a relenting look.

I slipped into the car and locked the doors before I called Alex.

"Kate?" he asked, his voice strained. "Are you—"

"I'm free to go," I said quickly.

"Good. Okay. That's good." He breathed deeply, then said, "Listen, let's have a few rules in this relationship. Never request to be bailed out then hang up. It's not good for my heart."

"I'm sorry. I didn't want to tick off the policeman by talking on my phone while he was waiting."

"I'm afraid you're going to have to talk to him again tonight," Alex.

"Why? What happened?"

"I went back to the Royal Palms Resort bar and met the woman who is calling herself Harriet Hayden."

"The woman who is calling herself Harriet?" I repeated slowly. "You mean she isn't Harriet?"

"No. It took quite a few drinks to get the whole story, but she's definitely not Harriet."

I didn't love the idea of Alex plying another woman with drinks under a tropical night sky, but I pushed that thought aside for now. "But how can you be sure?"

"I saw her passport. Her real one, as well as the fake."

"She had two passports? You'd better start at the beginning."

"Right. Well, she certainly resembles Harriet, and she has a passport in Harriet's name. But she also has what she said was her own passport with the name of Nina Boydett. She's an actress. I looked her up online, and she has several stage credits and a few commercials. A few months ago, she got an email offering her a part, the part of Harriet vacationing in the islands. It was pitched as an elaborate reality show. She made it through 'the final cut' for the show. Then she received a package in the mail with the passport and credit cards in Harriet's name as well as instructions on what days to travel and information on her reservation at the Royal Palm Resort. Nina was convinced that hidden cameras were filming her and other guests at the resort."

"So who hired her?" I asked as I watched one of the officers wave Bridgette into the house. She and Carrie exchanged a long look as Bridgette walked into Harriet's house.

"Nina doesn't know. She has never spoken to a person about this. It was all handled through email. She was told that it was all very hush-hush. That it had to be that way to maintain the integrity of the filming."

"Alex, this isn't good. Harriet may have never left England after all."

CHAPTER 7

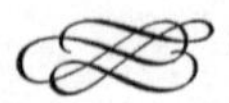

THE NEXT MORNING, AS I returned from walking Slink, I saw a police car parked in the village in front of the pub. Slink slurped water, then collapsed contentedly on her cushion while I found my gloves in the little storage space under the stairs. The day was even colder than yesterday, and a few snowflakes were drifting down from a dense layer of gray clouds. I had spent a restless night, thinking about poor Harriet. How awful to be missing for months and not have anyone notice, except a grocery store clerk. Of course, it seemed Harriet led a fairly isolated life, retreating into her writing and emerging occasionally to interact with fans and friends. But still, it was extremely sad.

By the time I reached the White Duck, the police car was gone. I half hoped there was some news, but I also dreaded what I might hear. I knocked on the door. Even though it was early, I knew Louise would be in, preparing for the day. She wasn't closing for the holidays until tomorrow, Christmas Eve.

She peered out through the diamond panes of glass and relief flooded her face when she saw me. She had a cell phone pressed to her ear and tucked it up next to her shoulder as she unlocked the door and let me in. She was speaking and waved me inside, then locked the door behind me. "Right. Yes, I know it's Christmas," she said sharply, and I gave her a long look. Her face was pale and her hand gripped the phone so tightly that her knuckles showed white. "I wouldn't call if I didn't need him. I understand it's not his area. Just have him call me please. Today. This morning."

She punched a button to end the call and rubbed her hand over her forehead. "Solicitors. Be careful what you wish for, Kate," she said in a weary voice. "I should know that by now, but I never seem to remember things like that until it's too late."

"What happened? Is it Gina?" I asked.

"No. There's been no change in her condition. I checked this morning, first thing." Louise pulled a chair out and collapsed into it. "We wanted the police to look into Harriet, take her possible disappearance seriously. They certainly are now."

"So Alex must have gotten through to the right people," I said. After I'd talked to Alex yesterday, I'd spent quite a while trying to convince the police at Harriet's house that they needed to talk to him. He had already spoken to the police on the island, but they were reluctant to get involved until requested to do so by the U.K. authorities.

"I'll say. They've searched Harriet's house. No sign of her...or of a struggle or anything like that."

"Yeah, when I was there, everything was neat and exact," I said, thinking of the cleared desktop and the spotless kitchen.

"But they've found her will, the police informed me this morning. The case has been bumped up to a DCI," she said with a roll of her eyes. "And not that nice young man who investigated those last incidents. This is an older man with very cold, accusing eyes."

"Surely, he's not looking at you as a suspect?"

"But he is. It was quite plain."

"Why? You have no reason to hurt Harriet."

"It's because of her will. He said there was a copy of it in her files. Gina is to receive three-hundred-thousand pounds."

I blinked. "That's quite a bit of money." With the current exchange rate, that was nearly half a million dollars. "Wow. I had no idea Harriet made so much money."

"I told you her books sold well," Louise said, her voice impatient.

"But that doesn't mean *you* have a motive."

"The book club meeting is the last trace he's found of Harriet. Gina and I were the last people to see Harriet alive. The DCI thinks Gina knew about the will, and that Gina and I killed her, planning to split the money."

"But that's absurd. Anyone who knows you, would know you would never—"

"Well, the DCI *doesn't* know me, and I have the feeling he's moving as quickly as possible on this thing to make up for lost time. It can't look good for them, that they ignored Gina when she told them Harriet might be missing. No, he wants to tidy up this case and get it off the books."

"But if you and Gina...did away with Harriet, why would Gina try to convince them to look for Harriet?"

"According to the police, Gina must have had a guilty conscience and wanted the truth to come out. I poisoned her to keep her quiet. At least, that's what the police insinuated. It's the only thing that explains both Harriet's disappearance and Gina's poisoning, he said."

I sat there, trying to think through the convoluted scenario. It could have been possible, just barely, but it was all wrong. "That's just...crazy."

Louise shrugged and stood, replacing the chair. She gave the table a swipe with a cloth that she pulled from her pocket. "Well, that's the way it is, at least until I can get through to the solicitor." She turned and walked toward the bar, her shoulders sagging. "I have invoices I need to pay."

I trotted along behind her, thinking furiously. "Is Gina the only beneficiary? And why did Harriet leave money to Gina in the first place?"

"I don't know. He said there was some statement in the will about how kind Gina was and her love of books and reading, but honestly, I zoned out there for a moment. All I know is she stands to inherit a lot of money."

"What about the house? Does Harriet own it?"

"I don't know."

"And the rights to her books? Who gets those?"

"I have no idea." Louise rearranged some glasses behind the bar.

"But it could be important."

Louise drifted to the chalkboard and erased the day's specials as I spoke. She picked up the chalk but stood there staring at the board.

"It could mean more motives," I said. "I bet the rights to Harriet's books are worth way more than a couple hundred pounds. We're talking continuous income as long as the books sell. We need to see that will and—"

Louise's phone rang. She answered quickly. After listening for a moment, she said, "Of course. I'll be there as soon as I can." She ended the call. "Gina is awake and asking for me."

I STAYED in the waiting room while Louise went to see Gina. Louise had called Ella to cover the pub again, and because Louise was so flustered and nervous, I'd driven her to the hospital. I needed to go to Upper Benning anyway. The shop owner had called that morning with the news that Alex's print was in.

At the hospital, the nurse informed us that only one person could see Gina, so I'd left Louise and driven the short distance to the Christmas market. The festive atmosphere was exactly the same, but I felt disconnected from it and couldn't enjoy it. The print was in good shape and beautifully framed, so the owner wrapped it up for me and, after gulping at the overnight shipping charge, I paid him then hurried through the cheerful crowds. I managed to wedge the print into the MG, but I wasn't sure if I'd be able to get both the print and Louise in the car for the return trip to Nether Woodsmoor.

At the hospital, I was too antsy to stay in the uncomfortable chairs. I paced around the waiting room for a few moments, but it was so stuffy that I went outside and took a brisk walk through the rows of cars to the far edge of the parking area. The air was crisp, and snowflakes spun lazily in the air. Through a gap in the buildings, I could see a bit of the rolling countryside. The edges of the fields near the dry stone walls that criss-crossed the land were already white with snow.

I retrieved my camera from the car and snapped a few photos as my thoughts spooled. During the drive to the hospital that morning, Louise and I had talked through the possibilities of why someone would want Harriet out of the way. Since she didn't seem to have any sort of close relationship—no boyfriend or lover—that seemed to rule out a crime of passion or jealousy. And the police seemed to agree with their close focus on Louise and

Gina. So that left money…or an inheritance. We needed to find out who else would benefit from Harriet's death.

I returned to the close atmosphere of the waiting room and found Louise emerging from the elevator, her face strained. "That DCI had already been in to see Gina." She gripped my arm. "He tried to get her to admit to murdering Harriet. He'd checked up on Gina and found out she has missed her last two house payments. I had no idea. She never said a word to me until today, but they cut back on her hours at the grocery, and there are rumors of a reduction in staff."

"Which explains why the police are looking at her as a suspect. Financial troubles combined with the fact that she was one of the last people to see Harriet alive…well, that's not good."

Louise gripped my arm. "She's so weak. She looked just awful, and now she's terrified she'll be arrested." Louise checked her phone. "Why doesn't the solicitor call? He doesn't know it, but he has two clients now." She ran a trembling hand over her forehead, pushing up her bright bangs. "At least I have a little money saved. I won't be able to update the pub's kitchen, but, well, if I'm not in prison, I guess it will be money well spent."

The thought of Louise spending money to defend herself from these ridiculous insinuations made me fume. "Louise, I know you didn't do anything to harm Harriet. Do you think there's even the *remotest* chance that Gina had something to do with Harriet's disappearance?"

Louise instantly shook her head. “No. Gina is a gentle person. I know you saw her get agitated over Harriet’s disappearance, but no matter how difficult her life is, she would never, ever do anything like that.”

“Okay, then let’s find another suspect for the DCI.”

CHAPTER 8

I RANG THE DOORBELL AT Harriet's house and stepped back. Louise waited a few steps behind me. I'd often been in this situation as a location scout, cold calling, asking for something from someone who had no reason to even speak to me. I felt that same frisson of nervousness that I always did, but I forced myself to ignore it. A lot more was riding on this conversation than a filming location.

The door cracked open, and Bridgette peered out. I hoped she'd be there. She didn't have anywhere else to go.

"Hi, Bridgette. I'm sure you're not really in the mood to talk to anyone today with the news about your sister, but I think you might be able to help us figure out what happened."

"The police know what happened. They told me this

morning that they think some clerk at the grocery did it, for money."

"And the police never get anything wrong, do they? They never have the wrong idea about anyone."

After a long pause, Bridgette opened the door wider. "What do you want?"

"Do you have a copy of Harriet's will? That would help."

She looked at Louise. "Who's this?"

"I'm Louise, a friend of Harriet's."

"I remember you from the market. Okay, come in." Bridgette walked to the kitchen where she motioned for us to take the two seats at the counter.

She'd showered and had on fresh clothes. Her hair was pulled back in a ponytail, which only emphasized her puffy, red eyes. She picked up a folded stack of papers from the desk and tossed it on the counter. "That's her will."

"I thought the police had it." I smoothed out the creases as I opened it.

"Harriet had another copy. Of course she did. That's Harriet all over. Always prepared. I mean, she even has a list of her passwords, right there stuck to her laptop keyboard. Alphabetized, too. Go on, read it if you want, but all the legalese boils down to two things. This Gina person gets some money. I get everything else—the house, the contents, and rights to her books—but only *after* I go through rehab." Bridgette looked away, her eyes glistening. "Typical Harriet. Bossy, even in her will."

"But that's what you wanted," I said.

"Yes. I'm going to do it as soon as...well, as soon as all this is sorted." She gestured at the papers in my hand. The doorbell rang. "I'd better get that. Might be the police again," she said with a small smile in my direction.

I had put the will down, but Louise picked it up and scanned the print. "She's right. She gets everything else." Louise gave me a significant look. "That sounds like motive to me."

"Yes, although she said she just arrived here," I said as the murmur of two female voices floated back to us.

"You told me yourself she said she was an addict." Louise kept her voice low.

I'd filled Louise in on what Bridgette had told me. I hadn't kept anything from Louise. I knew she could keep a secret, and she was the one being questioned by the police. It only seemed fair that she have all the information.

"To get their next high, addicts will do whatever they have to," Louise said in an urgent whisper. "Where was she a few weeks ago? If she knew about the will, she could have killed Harriet, knowing she'd have a steady income from her books for years and years."

"Then where's the body?" I asked. "It would be much easier to inherit if Harriet's body was found."

"Something must have happened. Maybe she put it somewhere where she thought it would be found, but it hasn't been, and that's why she's here now."

The volume of voices increased. Something else was

bothering me about what Louise said. "A steady income," I murmured. "Someone else has been profiting from Harriet's disappearance."

"What do you mean?"

"Who is selling Harriet's autographed books at the market?"

"Carrie," Louise breathed. "Yes, you're right." She lowered her voice another notch. "Speak of the devil."

Carrie swept into the kitchen. Dressed in yoga pants and a hooded sweatshirt, she looked quite different than she had in her Regency outfit. "I'll just pop these in here for you. I don't cook," she said with pride, "but these takeaway dinners are absolutely delicious."

She entered the kitchen. Her steps faltered when she saw Louise and me. "Oh, I didn't know you had company. Louise." She sent a minuscule smile in our direction, then spotted the papers on the counter. She had a difficult time looking away from them as she placed several white containers in the refrigerator.

"I won't keep you," she said to Bridgette. "If you need anything, anything at all, just pop over. Harriet and I were very close. I can't tell you how sad I am to hear the news. So tragic."

A crazy thought came into my head, and I missed Bridgette's reply as I debated if I should do it. It was a risk. But when would there be another chance? And the police seemed to be so focused on Louise and Gina...

"Yes, it really is sad," I said, a little too loudly.

Everyone looked toward me. I cleared my throat. "I

know it's a personal loss for all of you, but there are her readers, too. They'll be devastated to hear the news." I turned to Louise. "No more books from their favorite author. And the book club will never get to read that last book she was working on. Or any of the others she had planned, those she told the book club about." Louise opened her mouth, but I kicked her lightly in the shin. "You know, the ones on the flash drive that she always kept with her."

Under her bright bangs, Louise's forehead wrinkled. "I don't think that's what matters right now—" she began.

I cut her off. "Not to you or Bridgette, of course. You'll miss Harriet herself. And that's what's important, but later...her readers will want to know what happened in the series." I said to Bridgette, "Later, when you go through her things, you'll have to look for a flash drive with her last story and her novel outlines. She told the book club all about it, didn't she, Louise? How she didn't like online backups...that she preferred to keep it with her."

"Yes, she mentioned that," Louise said slowly.

"Maybe the flash drive is here." I glanced toward the desk.

Bridgette shook her head. "No, the police didn't find anything like that. I saw the list of items they took."

"Anyway, something to think about," I said. "We really should go. We've stayed long enough. Thank you for talking to us, Bridgette."

I hurried Louise along the hall and had us across the

brick pavers before Bridgette or Carrie could catch us. Louise opened the passenger door. "What was all that about? Her readers are the last thing we need to be thinking about now."

"No, I think that's really the main thing." I slid into the car seat and motioned for her to do the same. Once she was inside the car and wedged up against Alex's print, I said, "Or, her books, to be specific. Of all of her estate, her literary works are the most valuable. And what happens to artists' work when they die? Often, the demand goes up. Limited supply, you know. Imagine if in a year or so, the last of Harriet's books came out? The demand would be high. But if she had outlines for future books…well, a ghostwriter could complete them."

"And that would mean more income on top of what is already coming in from her books now," Louise said. "But she never said anything about outlines of future books."

"Yes, I made that up." I started the car and pulled away from the curb. "Just a little added incentive. I hope it wasn't too over-the-top, but I guess we'll find out."

"IT'S BEEN FOUR HOURS," Louise said.

Only Louise's head showed above the framed print, which we'd managed to angle into the car between the seats with most of it on her side of the car so that I could operate the gearshift. "I know, but it's only been fully dark for about an hour. If I were going to dig up a body, I'd wait until it was dark."

"Thank goodness the days are short this time of year," Louise said. It was only five, but it felt much later.

After we left Bridgette and Carrie, we cruised Harriet's neighborhood until we found a good vantage point at the end of the road, a block north of Harriet's street. Alex's red MG Midget was cute, but definitely too memorable to park on Harriet's street. The street we decided on was at a slightly higher elevation, and we could see into the back gardens of both homes as well as enough of the street in front of her house, so that if either Bridgette or Carrie left, we'd be able to see them.

"I need the loo," Louise said, a couple of hours later.

"I know. Me, too." Earlier in the day we'd taken turns walking down the residential street to the nearby row of shops for food and bathroom breaks, but now it was fully dark and after ten. I doubted anything adjacent to the quiet residential area would be open. The lights had gone out on Harriet's side of the building around nine-thirty, but Carrie's windows were still bright.

"Sorry again about the print," I said. "Now I wish I'd bought Alex that wallet. I think he'll like the print, but it's not really that personal, is it? Maybe I should get him something else as well."

Louise turned toward me with an exasperated sigh. "Alex is crazy about you. It doesn't matter what you get him. You said so yourself, possessions don't matter to him. If you just kiss him under the mistletoe, he'd be happy with that."

"So you're saying I'm blowing this present thing way out of proportion?" I sighed. "You're probably right. I have a tendency to do that—"

"Did you see that?" Louise asked.

"No."

"I thought—yes, there it is again. Someone is moving around in Harriet's back garden."

"Okay. Here we go." I handed the keys to Louise and checked the settings on my camera one more time so that they let in as much light as possible. "Your phone is on, right?" I asked.

"And fully charged. Don't worry, luv. I'll call that snotty DCI the moment it looks as if she's trying to move...Harriet."

"Okay, here goes." I drew in a deep breath and slipped out of the car. After hours of sitting in one position, my legs felt stiff. The cold didn't help, but I managed to move to the front of the car and get in position without making any noise. I settled the camera on the hood of the car so I'd have a steady shot, then zoomed in on Harriet's garden. A little ambient light from several streetlights filtered into the yard, but it was still very dark. The snow had tapered off and a couple of little piles in the corners of the garden helped reflect a bit more light. The person wasn't facing me, and wore a hooded coat or sweatshirt, so I couldn't see the person's face.

Faintly, I heard the sound of a shovel slicing through

earth. It sent a chill through me. It had worked. Someone had taken the bait. With the camera sounds muted, I took several photos, but I was afraid I didn't have anything distinctive.

I removed the camera from the car's hood and crept back to the car door. Louise had lowered the window a few inches. I whispered, "I can't see who it is. You call the police. I'll try to get closer."

Louise's reply was barely audible. "I don't think that's a good idea."

"I'm not going down there, just to the edge of the little embankment over to the right that drops off above the garden. That should give me an angle that will let me get the person's face." Louise made a protesting noise, but I slipped away from the car and moved as noiselessly as possible.

Homes were under construction here, and the little cul-de-sac would be filled with homes later, but for now, most were cleared lots. I carefully picked my way through the dirt, pausing every few beats to listen. The sound of the shovel shearing through the earth continued.

I got close to the edge, where the land dropped a few feet down to the back garden below. I squatted down and peered through the viewfinder. This angle was better, and a patch of snow reflected on the figure. I snapped a few pictures, then my heart thumped faster as a swath of pale hair fell out of the hood.

The figure made an impatient movement, pushing

the hair away and the hood fell partially back. I held the camera steady, snapping off silent shots as Carrie looked up from the little mound of dirt, and surveyed the rise of land above her. I bit my lip and forced myself to hold the camera perfectly still in front of my face. After a second, the shoveling resumed, and I let out a shaky breath.

I slowly crept backward. It felt like it took forever to cross the empty lots. As I stepped from the dirt to the asphalt of the road, I realized that the steady, rhythmic sound of the shovel moving through dirt had stopped. I hesitated. Should I go back? No, I had enough on film, and the police should be on their way.

I was almost back to the car when a shadow seemed to move at the edge of my vision. I turned toward it and couldn't help letting out a shriek. Even in the dim light, I could see her. Carrie stood there, chest heaving, a spray of dirt on her face, and the shovel gripped like a baseball bat.

I held up a hand. "Wait, Carrie. Let's, um..."

She didn't hesitate. She tensed her arms as if getting ready to swing at a ball, but she was aiming for my head.

I fumbled for my camera, managing to click on the flash and aim it at her, snapping a series of blinding shots as a shadow shifted beside Carrie. Something big and dark came down on her upper back, thrusting her forward. She lurched and fell, hitting her head hard on the asphalt as pieces of broken wood and shards of glass rained down around her.

"Oh, Kate. I'm so sorry about the print," Louise said. "It was the only thing I had."

"No, that's okay." I reached for the bumper of the MG and lowered myself onto it. "Small trade-off for not being hit in the face with a shovel."

CHAPTER 9

"AND YOU GOT IT ALL on film," Gina said. "Louise rescuing you."

"Yes, she certainly stopped Carrie in her tracks." Gina was propped up against a pile of pillows on the hospital bed. She still looked pale and fragile, but her eyes were lively and alert.

Louise said, "The flash distracted Carrie while I got out of the car. If you hadn't done that," Louise broke off and cleared her throat. "She would have come after me with the shovel, too. And the print was no match for the shovel, even if the print was framed." Louise grimaced. "I still feel bad about that."

"Don't worry about it. The frame protected the print pretty well. It's just a little crumpled on one side. And sort of folded. But it will be fine, I'm sure."

"So what happened with Carrie? Did she wake up?" Gina asked.

"Not at that moment, thank goodness," I said.

"She'd hit her head pretty hard on the way down." Louise lowered her head and gave Gina a look. "Like someone else I know."

Gina gingerly touched her head. "Yes, I don't recommend it."

"Anyway, she was coming around when the police arrived," Louise continued. "But we explained what she'd been doing. They didn't seem convinced at first, even with Kate's photos to back us up, but after one look in Harriet's garden, they took Carrie away in the back of a police car."

"She'll face murder charges," I said, and Gina's animated face saddened.

"I hate it that I was right about Harriet. I didn't want to be, but deep down, I knew it. I knew she was dead." She shivered. "I can't believe Carrie buried Harriet in the garden. She was there, the whole time, and no one missed her."

"You did," Louise said. "You must have rattled Carrie with your questions. The mistletoe had to be her, didn't it? She poisoned you?"

Gina nodded. "Yes, the DCI came this morning. His manner was very different from last time. He was quite willing to answer all my questions. I have a lot of questions, you know." She smiled faintly. "They found traces of mistletoe on her Regency pelisse. The mistletoe was there at the market, a decoration. She must have crushed some berries and managed to slip them into my tea before the server brought it to us. They found the girl who delivered the drinks, and she remembered a woman who looked like Carrie bumping into her, but she couldn't remember exactly when it happened, or who she was serving at the time." Gina's gaze dropped to her hands. "I don't understand it, at all, but I suppose since Carrie had killed Harriet, she probably didn't have a second thought about dropping those berries into my tea." She smoothed the edge of the blanket over her lap. "The DCI said they believe she drugged Harriet and then suffocated her."

"Oh, that's awful," Louise said.

"They're doing tests and won't know for certain until the results are back, but the DCI said that Harriet didn't have any visible wounds, except for some bruising on her face around her nose and mouth." Gina shook her head. "Why would Carrie do that? What drives someone to be so cruel?"

"Greed," I said. "You said it yourself when you told me about Carrie. You said nothing was ever enough. She must have realized that Harriet was making a good income with her books. A look at Harriet's Facebook account would have told her about the upcoming trip. Carrie saw it as an opportunity to get rid of Harriet."

"They had traded keys," Gina said. "I know that."

"Right," I said, "so she hired an actress to play the part of Harriet to extend the fiction that Harriet was still alive. My friend Alex found out all about that. He also found out from the police in the Canary Islands that

Carrie was removing cash from Harriet's accounts, just as you thought."

Gina nodded, her face sad. "I wish I had been wrong."

"She had Harriet's purse and all her bank cards," I continued. "Bridgette said Harriet had a list with all her passwords in her desk. She'd gotten into Harriet's computer and redirected the funds. I think the only reason she stayed so long was to create an alibi for herself and keep an eye on Harriet's garden to make sure the body wasn't discovered. If the body was found, the process to shift all of Harriet's accounts to the beneficiaries would begin, cutting off Carrie's cash flow," I said.

"So as long as Harriet was on holiday, Carrie was safe," Gina said.

"The police in the Canary Islands have already found several emails between Carrie and the impostor she hired," I said. "I suppose Carrie planned to have the woman playing the part of Harriet mention her intention of touring some of the other Canary Islands. If 'Harriet' sent word back that she had extended her vacation again, then it would be easy for the fake Harriet to drop out of sight and make it much more difficult to track her down."

"And Carrie could go on collecting the earnings from Harriet's royalties," Gina said.

"Which is why Kate's mention of the flash drive with outlines of future books was so brilliant," Louise said. "Of course Carrie would want something like that."

"I wish that part of the story were true," Gina said. "I'd love to read another of Harriet's books."

"Well, it was partly true," Louise said. "Bridgette called me this morning. She'd looked through Harriet's computer before the police arrived this morning." Louise handed Gina a stack of papers. "She found a file labeled *Valentine Novella*. She sent it to me, and I printed it out for you."

Gina grinned. "Oh, Harriet did keep her promise. We will get one more Harriet Hayden story. I'm so glad. And, this sister, Bridgette, the police made her sound quite the shady character, but it seems she's trying to do the right thing."

I exchanged a look with Louise as I said, "She's had a rough time, but I think she'd already determined to change her ways before all of this."

Louise nodded. "She leaves tomorrow for rehab."

We chatted a bit more, but Gina's gaze kept straying to the printed pages, so when the nurse arrived, Louise and I said goodbye. Gina was already halfway through the first page before we were out the door, despite the nurse taking her vitals.

Outside the hospital, Louise said, "I still have Christmas shopping to do. Fancy another trip to the market?" The snow had begun to flutter down again but with more intensity than yesterday's snow. It was quickly coating everything in sight.

"No, my shopping is finished. I think I need to do some baking, then curl up with a good book."

Louise said, "If I don't see you before Christmas, thank you," and she gave me a quick, fiercely tight hug. "It goes without saying, doesn't it, that everything will always be on the house for you at the pub?"

"There's no need for that—"

"Yes," she said firmly. "There is. It's not much, but it's what I can do, and I don't want to hear any argument from you. It's Christmas, and it's not polite to refuse gifts."

I swallowed my arguments. "You're right. Thank you," I said sincerely.

"Right. Well. That's sorted then. Happy Christmas."

"Merry Christmas, Louise," I said, and handed her an envelope.

"What's this?" Her tone was suspicious as she pulled back the flap and extracted a card. "A spa day?"

"A little something—that you must accept," I said quickly, sensing that she was about to try to refuse it. "It's a gift. Must be polite and all. I think you'll love it. Massage included."

"A massage does sound heavenly," she said with a slow smile.

We said goodbye, and I managed to get back to my cottage in Nether Woodsmoor, only frightening myself a few times as the car drifted on the slick roads, seeming to have a mind of its own. I put the car in park with a sense of relief, returned Slink's energetic greeting, then whipped up a batch of sugar cookies.

I managed to get a fire going in the fireplace. Then I

settled into the couch near the blaze, a plate of cookies balanced on the arm of the couch, and *Miss Bingley Suspects* propped up on my knee.

The doorbell rang, and Slink went from horizontally sprawled on her cushion to vertical in milliseconds. I opened the door to see Alex standing there, snow rapidly building up on his hair. "Merry Christmas."

"What are you doing here? You're not supposed to arrive until the day after tomorrow."

Alex reached down to rub Slink's ears as she danced around us. "I wanted to give you this in person." He handed me a small wrapped package.

I could tell from the feel of it that it was a book.

"And I was worried about you," he continued. "Missing authors, impostors, poisoned tea. You know, not the typical Christmas."

"It all worked out…the whole thing. I called you yesterday, but I had to leave you a voicemail."

"That's because I was flying back. So, can I come in?"

"Yes, of course." I stepped back. "Sorry, I'm just so surprised to see you, but really glad, too"

"Yeah?"

"Yes." I put my arms around his neck. "Let me show you."

Eventually, we decided we should close the door. I was still holding the package, and as I shut the door, Alex brushed the snow from his hair as he said, "Go on, open it."

"Now? It's not even Christmas Eve."

"I won't tell."

I carefully pulled at the tape, trying to dislodge it without messing up the wrapping paper.

"I knew it. I knew you'd be one of those careful unwrappers," he said with a smile and crossed his arms as he made a show of leaning against the wall to wait for me. "Tick-tock. I could have opened all my presents in the time it's taken you to break that piece of tape open."

I punched his arm. "I'm not that bad." I pried the paper back and caught my breath as I recognized the peacock feathers. "A first edition of *Pride and Prejudice*." I ran my fingers over the embossed surface.

"Not a particularly good one, I'm afraid. It's worn. The technical term is 'foxed,' I learned, but I thought you'd like it."

"I do." I smiled wider. "Indeed I do," I said, reaching to give him a kiss.

I leaned back, remembering I had a gift for him. "Your present isn't wrapped." I nodded to the print, which was propped up on the couch. The frame was a total loss, but the cardboard backing on the print had only cracked in one place near the bottom of the print. I'd flattened it out and taped it into place. The print itself wasn't damaged that badly.

He crossed the room and picked it up, "This is...brilliant. I really like it."

"You do?"

"Yes. I don't have any proper art, so this is perfect." He

ran his hand over the crumpled edge that had connected with Carrie's back. "What happened here?"

"It's a long story. Come have some cookies while I tell you about it."

THE END

~

Stay up to date with with Sara. Sign up for her updates and get exclusive content and giveaways.

~

Don't miss Kate's next adventure in Nether Woodsmoor, Death in an English Garden, available in ebook, print, and audio.

A common, garden variety murder . . .

Location scout Kate Sharp is enjoying the gorgeous springtime in her favorite idyllic English village while coordinating locations for a Jane Austen documentary, but when she's assigned to manage a difficult star who has received threats, Kate discovers that danger and death aren't always on screen.

After a tragic accident in the star's beautiful English garden, Kate suspects murder. With a sly and secretive murderer intent on putting suspicion on Kate, she must find the culprit before she's led down the garden path.

Death in an English Garden is the sixth entry in the popular Murder on Location series from *USA Today* best-selling author Sara Rosett, which are perfect for cozy mystery readers who want to indulge their inner Anglophile.

THE STORY BEHIND THE STORY

Thanks so much for reading the *Menace at the Christmas Market* novella. I hope you enjoyed it. I always have fun writing Kate and Alex's adventures. I especially enjoyed exploring the world of Jane Austen fan fiction, which has an amazing array of titles available. It's so interesting to me that an author who lived two hundred years ago and wrote only six books continues to influence reading and publishing as well as pop culture. (There really are Jane Austen-inspired boy short panties, which I think would cause a few interesting comments from Austen!)

If you'd like to read more in the *Murder on Location* series, there are full-length titles available, *Death in the English Countryside, Death in an English Cottage, Death in a Stately Home, Death in an Elegant City, Death in an English Garden, and Death at an English Wedding*. I'm working on more books in the series. Sign up for my newsletter at SaraRosett.com/signup/2, and I'll let you know when a new book is out. You'll also get exclusive excerpts of upcoming books as well as access to member-only give-aways. Each novel in the Murder on Location series is a cozy mystery and explores some facet of Jane Austen, either the woman herself, her writing, or her influence in today's world.

ABOUT THE AUTHOR

USA Today bestselling author Sara Rosett writes fun mysteries. Her books are light-hearted escapes for readers who enjoy interesting settings, quirky characters, and puzzling mysteries. *Publishers Weekly* called Sara's books, "satisfying," "well-executed," and "sparkling."

Sara loves to get new stamps in her passport and considers dark chocolate a daily requirement. Find out more at SaraRosett.com.

Connect with Sara

www.SaraRosett.com

OTHER BOOKS BY SARA ROSETT

THIS IS SARA ROSETT'S COMPLETE library at the time of publication, but Sara has new books coming out all the time. Sign up for her newsletter to stay up to date on new releases.

Murder on Location — English village cozy mysteries

Death in the English Countryside

Death in an English Cottage

Death in a Stately Home

Death in an Elegant City

Menace at the Christmas Market (novella)

Death in an English Garden

Death at an English Wedding

High Society Lady Detective — 1920s country house mysteries

Murder at Archly Manor

Murder at Blackburn Hall

The Egyptian Antiquities Murder

Murder in Black Tie

An Old Money Murder in Mayfair

Murder on a Midnight Clear

Murder at the Mansions

On the Run — Travel, intrigue, and a dash of romance

Elusive

Secretive

Deceptive

Suspicious

Devious

Treacherous

Duplicity

Ellie Avery — Mom-lit cozy mysteries

Moving is Murder

Staying Home is a Killer

Getting Away is Deadly

Magnolias, Moonlight, and Murder

Mint Juleps, Mayhem, and Murder

Mimosas, Mischief, and Murder

Mistletoe, Merriment and Murder

Milkshakes, Mermaids, and Murder

Marriage, Monsters-in-law, and Murder

Mother's Day, Muffins, and Murder

Printed in the USA
CPSIA information can be obtained
at www.ICGtesting.com
LVHW042247290723
753836LV00007B/241